Alan Bissett

The Ching Room
&
Turbo Folk

Salamander Street

PLAYS

First published in 2021 by Salamander Street Ltd.
(info@salamanderstreet.com)

The Ching Room © Alan Bissett, 2009

Turbo Folk © Alan Bissett, 2010

ISBN: 9781913630997

Printed and bound in Great Britain

10 9 8 7 6 5 4 3 2 1

For David MacLennan,
enjoying the great gig in the sky.

Contents

The Ching Room

First performed as part of the A Play, a Pie and a Pint series

Òran Mór, Glasgow, March 2009

Directed by Cheryl Martin

DARREN Andy Clark

RORY Colin McCredie

Darren   ## Rory

Sir?

                                   Oh! Sorry, I didn't think anyone was in here.

Quite alright, sir, easy to mistake to make.
In you come.

                                               Okay, thanks.

                                               Uh…

Sir?

                        Well, I can't get in until you come out.

I see, sir.

                                    Were you about to go?

No, sir, no. I've gone.

                                        Okay then.

I'm *well* gone.

              In which case could you maybe…uh…leave me to it?

No can do, sir, no can do.

                                         Why not?

Because there's room for us both in here, sir.

                                  Room for us both…?
      Look, this is the only cubicle, and it's kind of an emergency, and
                 you're not *doing* anything, so if you don't mind….

Not doing anything? On the contrary, sir.
I am on official nightclub business in here.

                                   I don't understand.
            Why would you need bouncers in the cubicles?

Not a bouncer, sir, not a bouncer. Neither bruiser nor gorilla, I.
My matters are more, shall we say, spiritual that that.

> Well if you're not a bouncer then what are you doing here?

Oh come now, sir, I think we both know.

> No. We really don't.

We're both aware what you're actually here for, sir.

> *I'm* here to expel several pounds of faeces from my arse.
> I don't know what you're here for.

Are you serious, sir? You don't know where you are?

> Em, a nightclub toilet?

Oh no, sir, no. Perish the thought.

> On Sauchiehall Street?

Not any more, sir.

> Okay then. Where am I?

Come away in, sir, come away in.
Helluva draught with this door open.

> Well, uh, I really should get back to my girlfriend.

I thought you said it was an emergency?

> Maybe I could nip across the road or something…

You're quite safe, sir.
This is a frequent problem I find in contemporary society, sir: *trust.*

Do you trust me?

Do you trust me?

> Em. Um. Sure.

Good. So come in.

> Okay.

> Okay…just for a second.

(click)

> What are you locking the door for?

No reason to be afraid, sir, I merely stand between you and it so we will not be interrupted by scum and lowlifes. I feel certain sir shares my distaste for many of the fiends and vagabonds who walk the dancefloors of this establishment, not unlike creatures of the night in many respects. Don't you agree, sir?

> Of course. Uh.
> You always have to be careful of…the wrong sort.

A crucifix and garlic one sometimes needs round here, sir! Now. Take a good look around. Is it coming to you?

> No.

Oh baffled little sir. You make my heart gay with your naïvety! You, sir, have found your way to a place many think to be a mere myth. More mysterious than Atlantis, more magical than Narnia, more dangerous than the Bermuda Triangle. This, sir?

This. Is the Ching Room.

> Ching room. What's a…what's a ching room?

Sir. Again you wound my sensitive feelings! Not 'a' Ching Room, sir, *the* Ching Room. Capital 'C', capital 'R'. Such are the ways in which it is differentiated from the many thousand inferior, knock-off ching rooms in nightclubs up and down this great nation of ours, run by toe-rags who believe in grubby material profit more than they do the quality of the great and holy Ching.

This, sir, is the room from which Ching first did emerge, spreading its word, from heart to heart. The cradle, if you will, of civilisation.

> Ooookay.
> And you are…?

I, sir, am a mere servant of the Ching. Its priest, if you like. Its representative here on Earth.

I've really got to get back to my girlfriend.
It's her birthday, you see, and she's already upset
that I announced quite loudly to her friends
that I needed a 'Number Two'.
Had quite a bit to drink, you see.
And this is all starting to make me feel a little bit...uh...

I'm sorry, sir, but once the threshold to the Ching Room has been crossed
a transaction must take place, or else the cosmic balance of the Ching is
disrupted. Do you want to be responsible for that, sir? Do you want to be
responsible for tampering with the natural laws of the universe?

No, um. Of course not.

No.
I didn't think so, sir.

Trust has been given and most gratefully received.

Now you and I have what's known in the business as
'the business'
to get down to.

Business?

Official Ching Business.

Look, I really don't understand what's going on here, and the thing is,
the thing is...I've left my jacket out there
and the problem with some of my girlfriend's crowd is
well they're a rougher sort than you or I –
and one of them's known to be a bit of a 'tea-leaf', y'see?
Different to my previous girlfriends, this one.
Anyway my jacket is from Top Man, so I'd really hate to lose it,
and I think you can appreciate why I *really* need to get back out there.
Ha ha ha.

Ha ha ha!

Got ourselves in with a rough crowd, have we, sir?

Well, they are an *earthier* lot than I'm perhaps used to, yes.

Wee bit out of our depth in a venue like this, are we, sir?

6

Quite. One of those things.

Far cry from Hogwarts, is it not, sir?
I did warn you about the type of lowlife *tramp*
who frequents this establishment, did I not?

Tramp? No hang on.
That's my *girlfriend* we're talking about.

Take it up the arse, does she, sir?

Excuse me?

That crowd of hers out there.
Mainly men, is it?

Well, yes, as it happens.

Ever stopped to wonder why that is, sir?
Make you feel somewhat inadequate?
You with your tiny, wee, middle-class goldfish member flopping away
inside her gigantic ravine....

Now listen here!
I *really* don't think you should talk that way about wome-

NO, YOU LISTEN, SIR!

Thank you.

Let me explain our so very cute little situation here, *sir*. There are certain,
shall we say, *metaphysical* issues you seem unwilling to face. You have
reached the final stage in the evening's and – let's not understate things
here – *mankind's* evolution. You have ascended the levels, dodged the
whirling chainsaws, leapt the chasms, and now, at last, you are ready to
face the Big Boss.

Big Boss?

Boss Ching.

Boss Ching. Right.
Could you just get out of the way of that door, so I could maybe...

When an architect, sir, first sat down to design this nightclub, he and
his poofy interior designer pals sipping their lattes, could never have

imagined that their vision would culminate in such an exclusive room as this. For only two people are allowed entry beyond the red ropes at any one time, sir, and those people are, at present, myself and yourself.

Boss Ching has arranged it thus.

Can I speak to Boss Ching?

Boss Ching will be here shortly, sir.

Can you tell me what he looks like?

He is a white man, sir.

Can you maybe ask him to hurry up? I kind of need to go.

Hurry up? You don't hurry up Boss Ching, sir. Boss Ching hurries *you*.

But –

If you'll *just* let me get a word in, sir. There are soldiers – brothers to the likes of you and I – on the frontlines of Iraq and Afghanistan who, as the Mujahideen rain Holy Jihad upon their candy asses, talk through the tears about journeying home, tasting the sweetness of their girlfriend's mouth again and, one day, with the help from Lord God Almighty, the only being above Boss Ching himself, visiting this very room.

Even those presently feeding worms in the graveyard have heard of us, sir. You and I could go there this evening, sprinkle some Ching across the graves, and turn the place into the fucking Thriller video.

But *first*, sir.

You and I have to do some business.

Well, I definitely have to do some business, so if you don't mind…

Sir. If *you* don't mind. Would I come to your place of work, take down my pantaloons, and shite right there in front of you while you talk to a customer? While you sell him mobile *phones*? No, sir. I would not. You'd probably kill whichever impertinent cunt did that, would you not, sir? Who embarrassed you in your business-life to such a degree, would you not, sir?

Well I –

WOULD YOU NOT, SIR!

> Uh.
> I suppose I'm....not needing to go...anymore.

Such are the healing properties of Ching.

Say, 'Thank you, Ching Room.'

> Thank you, Ching Room.

Ching Room says no problem at all, sir. Say 'Amen'.

> Amen.

We are mere vessels for the Ching.

> Uh, I'm sorry to insist upon this point, but can I just ask...

Sir?

> What is...?
> What is –

What is Ching?

> Exactly.

What is Ching, sir? What is Ching? This is the question which every man must ask himself on a Saturday night on the greatest boulevard the world has ever seen.

> Sauchiehall Street?

Indeed, sir. Washed and blessed with Ching.

Yet what is Ching? What is the condition of Ching?

Ching is like....coffee made from thunder, sir.

> Eh?

It will make you shit rainbows.

Accept the love of the Ching Room and you will be rewarded with nirvana itself, sir.

Refuse the Ching Room and it will enact...

a terrible revenge.

                                                                    I see.

What's it to be, sir?

Pain or love? The Ching room dispenses both.

                                            Okay, back up there, bud.

Sir?

                            Now just you wait. Just *hang on* a minute.

It is not advisable to dispense orders in the –

                            – in the Ching Room. Yes okay, I get it.

                            You're a drug dealer, aren't you?

That is but one of the roles which the Ching has chosen for me, sir.

But, like the Ching itself, I have many names.

                                            What's your real name?

Darren.

                                                                Darren?

Darren.

                                            Okay, *Darren*, hi.
                                            I'm Rory.

Nice to meet you, Rory.

                Can't say the same. Now listen, *Darren*. Have I got this correct?
I'm here to take what I can't refer to in any other way than 'a great big shit'.
You think I'm here to *purchase* some shit, but I'm too afraid to ask for it.
                        That's the misapprehension we're labouring under here.
                                                                Am I right?

That seems to be the case, sir, yes.

                And are you telling me that should I elect to purchase some...

Ching.

Ching, yes, I believe you called it *several* times.
Should I purchase some 'Ching' I'd be assured of a happy time
because the 'Ching' which *you're* selling is of a superior quality
to that being sold in toilet cubicles elsewhere?

It's like the difference between Take That and Beethoven, sir.

Oh, quite the snob.

Am I also right in saying that should I decline the 'Ching'
being so cryptically offered to me
that there may be some kind of...*violence*....
visited upon me in the near future?

I think we might finally be reaching an understanding, sir, yes.

How much does it cost?

Well, sir, price is something which it seems almost sacrilegious to attach
to a substance as pure and true as the Ching. It'd be like wandering into
the Sistine Chapel and asking the Pope how much it cost him to paint the
ceiling.

We're in a toilet on Sauchiehall Street.

I accept the reality of the situation, sir.

How much does it cost?

Seventy pounds a gram.

What? That's outrageous!

Scuse me a second, sir.

Ih?

That you, Barry?

Fuck ye want?

Aye, well I'm daein business in here, cunt!

Whit?

Just fuckin stab him.

Naw naw, nae mair negotiations, Barry. Sickay hearin it.

I dunno, cunto, yaize yer loaf!
Skin him alive if ye havetay, long as I'm paid.

Sorry for the interruption there, sir.

Some people, eh? Don't know the meaning of the phrase
'buying a dog but having to bark yourself.'

Where did we get to?

> …mumble mumble….

Seventy pounds, thank you very much indeed, sir. The Ching Room
welcomes you into its church. Now, if you'll just allow me to prepare the
sacrament.

> Was he, uh, was he a business associate of yours?

He'd like to think so, sir. But one prefers to think of him as something of
an…employee. Ronald McDonald doesn't flip burgers himself, does he,
sir? No, he has people to do that for him. Too busy with his children's
parties.

Like this one.

> Didn't he, ha ha…
> Didn't he read the job description?

You'd imagine so, wouldn't you, sir? They can be irritating when they
simply fail to do the tasks for which they were hired. I mean, there was
no mystery about it. Employee sought for up-and-coming new enterprise.
Unsociable hours. Occasional knee-cappings. There are laws protecting
workers from entering into contracts with employers where terms are
unclear. So I think I've kept myself in the right, don't you, sir?

> No troubles with the unions for you!

Quite.

Do you have difficulties with subordinates yourself, sir, in the, uh, bank…?

> I don't work in a bank.

The estate agent's then?

You're way off.

Would sir care to make it apparent what the fuck he does for a living?

I'm a poet.

Ah.

Sir.

A poet.

Now it's all starting to make sense.

Make much money doing that?

Out of poetry? You kidding?

Well we seem to be able to chuck seventy pounds
about without too much care.
Don't we, sir?

And that – what's his face? – that Dr Seuss has done alright out of it,
hasn't he?

I don't really publish that often.
I'm, uh. I'm a wedding poet.

A wedding poet?

Bear with me here, sir, I'm not exactly up to date on current trends
in the field of literature. My hands are a wee bit dirtier than that.
Could you maybe explain to me what it is exactly a wedding poet does?

Okay, well you know how some people become professional musicians
because they dream about being the next Jimi Hendrix or Kurt Cobain?

Here, sir.
The Ching can make those dreams into reality.

I'm sure it can.
Well simply wanting to be the next big thing doesn't pay the bills.

All have bills to be paid, sir. You're preaching to the converted.

So they join a band that does weddings.
Y'know, they play 'Wonderful Tonight' and the Proclaimers and

'Congratulations'.
Even if it's killing their soul, at least they're surviving on the thing they
love the most. Their music. Their art.

That's a rare thing, sir.

So…

I realised that there was a market out there for poetry at weddings.
A lot of couples have a wee recital during their ceremony and I can
write them a few lines. For a fee. For another fee I can even
come to their wedding and read it aloud for them.

That right?

Get plenty work from that do we, sir?

Enough.

I like that, sir. Entrepreneurship. Engine of the economy.
Little did I know you were one of my very own.
Allow me to express my sincere admiration.

Thanks.

Would sir maybe…?

No.

What?

No, it's silly.

What is it? Go on.

Would you maybe recite me one of your wedding poems?

Recite you one?

Just so I can understand the kind of thing sir means.

Well, I don't know.
The circumstances are rather unusual.

They are that, sir! On the other hand, the holy union of man and woman
under God is not – if you care to stretch your imagination – so different

to the transcendental union we shall soon feel under the benevolent gaze of the Ching.

I'd be most grateful.

Okay. Um. Let me see if I can remember one…

HO!

FUCK OFF, CUNT, THIS CUBICLE'S BUSY!

AYE? WANTAY START LIKE? YE WANT A FUCKIN KNIFE THROUGH YER JAP'S EYE?

Shitein cunt.

Sorry, sir. Please. Continue.

Right. Uh. This one's called 'October Rain'.

It did not rain on the day I asked

If you would be my bride

And it did not rain on the day I asked

If you'd keep me warm inside

And it did not rain on the day I asked

If you'd wed my heart to yours

And it did not rain on the day I asked

If you'd keep us safe and pure

And if it rains, today, my love

As I take your hand in mine

I'll stand there soaking wet with you,

Until the end of time.

Hmm.

Sir.

That's really quite.

Pish.

> I know. I *know*. But that's the stuff they want.

With all due respect, sir? If you read that at my wedding?
I'd jump up and down on your heid.

> You'd have every right to. But believe me, when that was read at their
> wedding? You could have surfed on the floods of tears.

No accounting for taste is there, sir?

> Seriously, I've poured my heart out in these poems in the past,
> put everything into them, and they usually take one read of it and go
> 'It's a wee bit…well…obscure.'

> So then I toss off something like 'October Rain'
> in four minutes and they go gaga.

> Philistines.

Still, though? You're contributing to somebody's big day, sir.
That's a privilege. Know what I'm saying?

> Their big day. You should see some of these weddings! Chavtastic.
> These big fat brides and their awful dresses
> and their pigshit-thick husbands and their bratty little white trash childr-

Quite the snob.

See, sir, I'd like to think if I was in your position. Know, with a university
degree and a gift with words? I wouldn't use them to patronise and
condescend to ordinary people, people maybe not quite as fortunate as
myself.

> I didn't mean that. I meant –

Two people fall in love, get married, they want their day to be perfect.
They're spending the rest of their lives together, they might want it to
begin with a wee bit of poetry that sums up their feelings simply and
clearly. Cos, y'know, sir, maybe the people at that wedding haven't got the
time or the inclination or the education to sift through the many layers
of meaning and symbolism and references to Percy Bysshe fuckin Shelley
which you worked into your initial draft.

I appreciate that, I was just –

Maybe they just want to look at their Gary and their Lisa up there and hear some words that make them go, 'Aww. Isn't that nice, Agnes? Til the end of time. And funnily enough, Agnes, it's raining the day. Dae ye see that? And that could've spoiled everything. But see that poem, he made it seem alright, know? Cos even if they're wet, they're wet the gither? Know, Agnes? Aw that was just right. Them words.'

Yes. I suppose you're right.

But also, let's not forget, sir, the standard of the poetry that you have visited upon the Ching Room here today. William McGonagall's got nothing on you, has he?

Okay okay.

The Ching Room hears all, sir.

It must remain untainted by cunts prostituting their art just for the fuckin money.

Maybe no as different to that wee girlfriend of yours as you think, eh no sir?

Probably not, no.

Now.

Since we're finished our wee English lesson.

Maybe you might like to sample some true poetry.

Here.

Oh you want me to…?

Indeed I do, sir. Indeed I do.

Man writes poetry to become closer to God, does he not, sir?
To become at one with his environment?

…in some ways…

Well. Here are some lines.

…how do I…?

17

I'll show you, sir. It's very easy.

Roll up a banknote like this. Not that you've got many of them handy at the moment.

Press one nostril like this, okay? Bend your head down.

Put the banknote in your nose, put your nose to the line, and...

Fffffffffff!

Ah!

that's the fuckin

Whoo!

Now, sir. Your turn.

Okay, I just...

That's it. Press your nostril.

and just...?

Put your nose down to the line, sir.

Yep.

I'll help you.

And now just.

Ffffff!

That's it, sir.

That's the spirit!

Oh.

Oh lord.

Oh lord indeed, sir.

Can you feel the Ching possess you?

This is.

                                          Um.

                                          Ooh!

You'll be speaking in tongues before you know it, sir.

Good stuff?

                     It's not. Uh. It's not an unpleasant sensation, is it?

Gets better, sir.

                                          Tingly.

Equips us with what we need to make our way in the world.

Allows us access to our truer selves. Unleashed. Uninhibited.

                                          Yes, it's rather…?

                                          It *is* rather.

                                          Isn't it?

You feel it, sir?

                                          I do.

You feel that power coursing through you?

                                          Oh yes.

That…poetry?

                                          Poetry. Yes.

                                          I'm a poet.

You are, sir.

You're the best fucking poet in the world.

                                          I am!

Rabbie fucking Burns, sir? He was an amateur.

                     I am a good poet! I'm a great poet.

                     Yeah. And none of them know it!

Don't appreciate genius, sir

                          Yeah. I'm an artist. What am I doing pissing around
                          with fucking weddings? I should be *published*.

Have another line, sir.

                                           Yeah.

                                         Fffff!

You like it?

                                   Wonderful!

Let's hear it now, sir.

                                      What?

Your poetry.

                                 My poetry?

Raw.

                                      Now?

Pure.

                                 Right now?

Uncut. Uncensored.

                                 Improvised?

Straight off the top of your head, sir!

                                 The real stuff?

Yeah! Feel it, sir. Deep in your soul!

                                     Yeah.

Tear it out of yourself!

                                     Yeah!

Fuck those bullshit weddings! Let me hear it. Let me hear it roar, sir!

Whoo!

My name is Rory. Now hear my story.

That's it!

My surname's Harris. I've been to Paris.

(beatboxing)

When I rock the mike it feels like the shit.
Took it to my homies and it was legit.

(beatboxing)

I'm here with my woman, she being a ho.

Ho!

Took it the Ching Room and Chinged with my bro!

Yo!

Rock!

(they both beatbox, then scat into…)

When you're on the Ching it's just the beginning and then pretty
soon you're actually singing cos the Ching soul brother's
a brand new beginning and the sinning and winning
is just what the Ching is.

Peace!

Yo yo yo.

Whoop!

My man!

Yeah!

You feel it?

Hell yeah!

Aye, it was still pish though.

You think?

Yeah. Total pish.

                        Oh. I was quite enjoying myself.

That's the main thing, sir. Ten out of ten for effort. We're getting there.

                        Yeah.

                        Good beatboxing, man.

Well. That'll be *my* arts education, sir.

                        Gotcha.

(Sniffs)

                        (Sniffs)

(Sniffs)

                        Any of that left?

In time, sir, in time.

                        (Sniffs)

While we're letting it all hang out, sir.
How did you end up with this wee girlfriend of yours?

                        How does anybody end up with anybody?
                        How did I end up here?

Pre-ordained, sir.

                        Ha ha. Quite.

But let's not avoid the question, eh?
Forgive me for saying, sir, but you don't seem very suited.

                        What do you mean?

'I'm here with my woman, she being a ho!'

                        Ho!

Kind of a wee clue.
Is it a sort across-the-tracks thing you've got going on with her?

You could say that.

And if I might be so bold, sir, I'm guessing she's a bit…younger than yourself?

Is it that obvious?

Well. I don't really think a club like this
is your, shall we say, natural habitat.

She's the babysitter.

Oh.

Sir.

Naughty boy.

My wife doesn't know.

Wouldn't imagine so, sir. Not the sort of thing one interrupts Coronation Street with an advert for, is it?

Let me just throw this out there, sir.
I'm guessing the wife's not a big fan of your poetry?

Well she's stopped reading any of it, so…

She does have some taste then.
None too fond of your cock either, sir, is she?

Hey.

Which makes the babysitter quite an attractive wee prospect, sir. That right? Flaunted herself a bit, didn't she? Tiny short skirts? Aye, I know the type, sir. We all know the type.

And I'm sure you don't make a habit of going out with her and her pals. That wouldn't be wise, would it? You mentioned something about a birthday. Have you and the wife have been dragged along? That why you're in a place like this?

Is your wife out there, right now? At the same table as her? And the wee girlfriend's getting a bit pissed, isn't she, and she's not being very subtle about thi –

No. My wife's not here.
She was going to come, but I told her not to.
Said it'd be full of kids.
I'd turn up, show face, stay for a drink, then bugger off.

And yet here we are in the Ching Room, sir. At a quarter past one.
Something's gone wrong with the plan. Something's forced you to stay.
Being a bit of a handful, is she?

Yes, well. Things aren't really…working out. Shall we say.

We shall say that, sir, if you wish. Speak to me, brother.

She has a… roving eye.

Ah, they all do, sir, they all do. Remember what I said to you? About the
basic problem of contemporary society?

What's that?

Trust.

This crowd of hers tonight. All these young boys.
Thinking they're men. All over her. And she's loving it.

And there's nothing you can do about it, is there, sir? Because you can't
break cover. And there's too many of them anyway, and they're harder
than you. And they're fitter than you, cos they're working boys using their
hands and muscles. And they're younger and better looking than you. So
you just have to sit there and take it, don't you, sir?

Fucking.

To *endure* it.

Little.

Am I right, sir?

Bitch.

Now now, sir.
Maybe you shouldn't talk that way about women

She chased *me*. She chased me for *so long*.

24

That's what they do, sir.

                                        I told her no. Time and time again.

Tut tut tut.

                        But every time she came back it'd be a lower cleavage,
                                                a flirtier wee glance.

                                        And then the texts started.

Texts, sir?

                                                                Look.

Oh.

Oh that's.

That's very.

Inventive.

I can see why a poet could appreciate writing like that.

Wasn't making it easy for you, sir, was she?

Ach, there's only so long you can go before you give in.
I understand that, sir. Any man can understand that.

                        And now she's joking about telling my wife.

Joking, sir?

            Except I know it's not a joke. She laughs about it, but I know what
                she's doing. She knows what she's doing. She uses it, every time
                                        she thinks I'm being too possessive.
                                                Like tonight.
            If she thinks I'm getting out of line, she'll just point to her phone.

                                        That's what she does.

You really think she'd do it?

                        Hell yeah. Yeah I do. She's young. She doesn't give a fuck.
                        She'd survive it, and I'd be blamed for the affair.

Sir's got himself into a bit of a mess, hasn't he?
Sir's housekeeping hasn't really been up to scratch.

                                            Tell me about it.

I'm with you, sir.

I am feeling it.

Let's take away this doubt and insecurity here, sir.
Why don't you let the Ching work its divine magic one more time, eh?
Go on. On the house.

                                              Thanks.

The Ching recognises a brother in pain. You accepted him in, sir.
You crossed the threshold and sealed the contract. The Ching Room
protects its own.

                                      Ffffffffff!

There you go, sir. That-a-boy.

                                              Whoah.

                                            This is.

                                              Whoah.

It's fine, sir, just ride it. Just ride into it.
Just let it take you. Let it be your friend.

Better?

                                              Better.

Let's lighten the mood now, eh? It's a Saturday, sir. The Ching Room's
Holy Day. Its Sabbath. We shouldn't dwell on the negative, sir. Not on the
Holy Day. Let's go back to a positive place.

                                        Yeah, please.

I want you to feel good about yourself, sir. The Ching Room wants you
to feel good about yourself. The Ching Room wants you to come back.
Again and again and again. This is why it provides the Ching. So what
I want you to do, sir, is I want you to recite to me the poem – any poem

– that you love most in the whole world. The one poem you wish you'd written. The poem that made you want to write poetry. That makes you transcend all these petty concerns.

                                                    You want me to recite it to you?

I do. I want to hear it, sir. I want to feel it.

                                                                              Sure.

                                        It's called 'Stopping By Woods on a Snowy Evening'
                                                                   by Robert Frost.

                                                          You really want to hear it?

Absolutely, sir.

                                        Well. I remember this from Primary School.
                                        Teacher read it to us. It was snowing outside.
                                                       Few days before Christmas.
                                        The whole lot of us still and listening.
                                                                        Her voice.

Let me hear it, sir. Let it come.

                        Whose woods these are I think I know.
                        His house is in the village though.
                        He will not see me stopping here
                        To watch his woods fill up with snow.

                        My little horse must think it queer
                        To stop without a farmhouse near
                        Between the woods and frozen lake
                        The darkest evening of the year.

                        He gives his harness bells a shake
                        To ask if there is some mistake.
                        The only other sound's the sweep
                        Of easy wind and downy flake.

                        The woods are lovely, dark and deep
                        But I have promises to keep.
                        And miles to go before I sleep.

                        And miles to go before I sleep.

Sir.

That was.

That was the most beautiful thing I've ever heard, sir.

You like it?

Like it, sir?

Words can't describe.

Yeah. Well.
I'll never get close to writing something as good as that.

But you *spoke* it, sir.

You spoke it and it went from you into me.

It passed between us.

That beauty.

Did you feel it?

I felt it.

You were the vessel for it. *You*, sir. That makes you powerful.

I suppose.

No, sir. No suppose about it. You moved me. You truly did.

It snowed on my wedding day, sir.

You were married?

Yes, sir. Hard to believe, isn't it? I remember waking up on the morning of it and… the snow…covering everything. All those filthy streets just made…white. The truth of that. It was like everything. Everything bad I'd ever done…was being purified.

By love. Like I was being….

Forgiven?

Forgiven, yes. I knew you'd understand, sir.

And she was really beautiful too, y'know? On the day.

Aye. I was very happy that day, sir.

Very happy indeed.

> I take it…it didn't work out?

No, it didn't.

> Right.

But that's fine. These wee problems go away. Eventually.

> Yeah.

Know something, sir? I'm really starting to quite like you.

> Ha. I'm starting to like me too.
> Finally.

See when you walked in here, sir, I thought: what does this poof know?
No offence, sir.

> None taken.

You just didn't look like you'd lived much, sir. That's all.

But see now?
I'm thinking maybe you've lived just as much as me.

We're the same.

You feel that, sir?

> I feel it.

That poem, man.

In fact, sir, in order to commemorate this moment.
I'd like to give you a wee gift.

> No, no, it's fine, I really couldn't take any more Ching.

It's not the Ching, sir. It's not the Ching. It's a gift *from* the Ching.
You get what I'm saying?

> Not really, no.

See these people out there, sir? These others? You don't need them.
The Ching Room speaks, and I hear what it says.
I'm its representative on Earth, see?

                                        I'm not following.

There'll be no repercussions.

                                  Repercussions to what?

The Ching Room can make this wee mistake of yours go away.

                          No, no don't do that, don't –

No no, it wouldn't do *that*. I thought we'd established already:
I'm a sensitive soul.
I sat there and appreciated your poetry, did I not?
I felt it move me. Deep inside.

This is what the Ching can do for you, sir.

It removes *doubt*.

It removes *all traces*.

                                  What are you proposing?

Oh, it's not me, sir.

It's the Ching Room. It makes the decisions here. But it does not like to
be refused. It does not like to be rejected. These are not fitting responses
to its love.

                                     What would happen?

Just a wee message sent. That's all.
Almost like a wee hello from the Ching Room.

There's a certain arrogance creeping into her behaviour, I'm sure you'll
agree, sir. People say that the Ching encourages arrogance, but it does
not. It corrects arrogance where it finds it. The same way in which we
have been humbled together here this evening.

You felt it too, sir. You told me you did.

                                              No traces?

Like snow.

And maybe if the Ching Room makes this wee problem go away, you might have to do something in return one day. Just a wee thing. Nothing that'll trouble you too greatly. Something…ceremonial.

Not much to ask for having your eyes opened, is it?

But you're not going to…to…

Sir. It's best not to wonder about the specifics.

Just a wee message?

In whichever form the Ching Room feels it appropriate to take, sir.

And all your troubles will just disappear.

Divine intervention.

Something like that, yes.

Right.

Now go back. Go back out there. And while you're sitting there listening to it all, watching them mock you and ignore you and disrespect you, you'll know.

Deep inside.

You'll feel that poetry.

That *power*.

Yes.

Yes.

Listen, man. Thanks for all of this.
It's been good to talk to someone about it.
Maybe I'll see you again?

I have no doubt, sir. Be waiting for me.

Oh and before you go?

What?

Don't forget your gram.
You paid for it, after all.

                                        So I did.

Goodbye, sir.

                                        Bye.

Say, 'Thank you, Ching Room.'

                              Thank you, Ching Room.

Say, 'Amen,' sir.

                                        Amen.

I remain your humble servant.

Sir.

END

Turbo Folk

First performed as part of the A Play, a Pie and a Pint series

Òran Mór, Glasgow, April 2010

Directed by Sacha Kyle.

VLAD Steven McNicoll

MIKO Simon Donaldson

CAMERON Ryan Fletcher

Cameron	Miko	Vlad

So this is the place where the locals hang out?
No tourists?

                              No tourists will come here.

Not surprised.
That street outside looked a bit shady.

"Say hey babe.
Take a walk on the wild side…"

                              No investment here.
                              Life difficult for many peoples.

What's this part of the city called anyway?

                              It doesn't matter.
                              You said come somewhere
                              you would not be recognised.

Aye it was a bit mad outside that hotel, eh.
I mean, have those girls not got homework to do?

                              Which girls?

Those wee fans waiting for me.
Trying it on as we were getting into the car.

                              They were not fans.

'Hey baby, we lovaz you.
We showz you za real good time, honey to za bee.'
Ach, they'll get over me.

But a bar like this, aye.
This feels *real*.

                              It is definitely real, sir.

Hey, Miko, I've told you,
there's no need to call me sir.

Where I come from people don't
stand on ceremony with each other.

Ah, then Scottish is good peoples, yes?

Yeah, we're a very…tolerant race.
Welcoming.
And when you think about it
there's no point you calling me sir
when we both work for the same company.

We do?

Aye. Just that one of us is in marketing
and the other is…the marketed.

I suppose that is true

So here we are…in the market-place.

Ha. We would not be able to sell you here.

Is it no your job to sell me anywhere?

Not while you are dressed like that.

Would you like drink?

Aye, cheers. Whisky please.

<Tva whiska, pallo.>

<Zaaar. Nae probz.>

Flavour?

What have they got…
Talisker. Macallan. Highland Park.
No a bad range.

Whisky popular here.

No wonder, when it's so cold outside!

Make it a Jura. Single malt.

<Zyik that yin, pallo.

Jura. Tva. Aye.>

<Zerya go, neebor.>

<Sanka.>

Just like being in the Drookit Duck.

Drookit Duck... is bar?
Of Scotland?

Aye, in Dundee. My home-town.
Good whisky, good company,
and if there's a ceilidh band playing
you get an awfully good racket.

Cay...lee?

Traditional Scottish music.
Drums, accordion.
Deedle eedle eedle.

Ah. The music of the people.

Aye, folk music.

It is harmless?

Well, I suppose you could be elbowed in the
face by a fiddler, but that's about it.

This music it is not
dangerous?

Think there's a wee problem with your English here, pal.
'Harmless' 'Dangerous.' It's just music. See what I mean?

Ah, but not all music
is just music.

Not according to the NME.

Enemy?

NME.

Enemy? Like gun? Bang bang?

For godsakes.
No, the N.M.E.
It's a *magazine*.

> Magazine! Ah of course,
> famous British NME.
> No more rock dinosaur!
> New look! New sound!

Exactly.

> Sorry, I mistake.
> Here we had *real* enemy.

You've never been reviewed by them.

> No, was guns. Bombs.

Aye, sorry, I shouldn't joke.
I know you've had troubles here.

> Yes, review. Let me remember.

> "Scottish singer-songwriter, Cameron
> McCann, reneges on his early promise with
> an album aimed squarely – and I stress
> "squarely" – at people who buy their music
> in ASDA. While McCann may be happy
> to hear one of these songs being butchered
> eventually on X-Factor, we can only hope
> that he rediscovers the spark that made his
> early singles so exciting. In the meantime,
> at least you know what to get your dad for
> Christmas."

> The NME. No?

Well remembered.

> Is job.

Still hurts.

> Is no guns and bombs.

No, suppose not.
Should look on the bright side eh.

> Yes. You are man who get up in morning,
> and play music.

But I mean, it sold! That's the main thing,
the bloody album sold!
Our mutual employer was happy.

> Very happy.
> I read emails from UK office.
> 'Throw party!
> Cameron McCann!
> Number ten in charts!'

Listen, that's not bad in an age when apparently
nobody wants to pay for music anymore.
Somebody needs to tell these critics:
you don't get to play the main stage at T in the Park
unless there's a lot of paying punters out there who love you.

> Drink to that.

Nice one. *Slainte*.

> Huh?

It's traditional. In Scotland.

> Ah okay. *Slainte*.
> Mm.

Good, isn't it?

> Is beautiful.

Hey, check out that barman's shirt.
That is one really cool shirt.

> Is also beautiful.
> But I prefer whisky.

Actually, I need to pick up something to wear
onstage tomorrow night.
Where do you think he might have bought that?

> Have no idea.

Hey, mate.

<Za?>

I like your shirt.

<Vit?>

Your shirt. I really like your shirt.

<Diznat spack Anglish, pallo.>

This. I like it. Thumbs up!

< Diznat teesh ma shyeert, cantyboz.>

Beautiful.

<Vit?>

WHERE DID YOU BUY IT?

I think now you should
leave him alone.

<Poofta.>

What's his problem?

He cannot understand you.

I just wanted to tell him he had a nice shirt.

Best to leave. Come.

Obviously no used to foreigners.

<Or bawbagz…>

What?

No. No foreigner here.

<Hey!
Chyiz!>

Em. Cheers!

Come. Jukebox play music.

40

You will like. This way.

A jukebox, aye?
What does it have on it?
Rock? Jazz? Blues?

Ah, is like music you say in
bar in Scotland.

Traditional?

Yes. Of the people.
Is folk. But volume? Turbo folk.

Turbo folk?

Like Bob Dylan. The electric.
"Judas!"

Oh right, I see.
Turbo folk. I like the sound of that.
Well, Miko, that's why I wanted to come out tonight.
New music, new experiences, all good for…
filling up the well.

Well is dry?

Not for long.
gmp!
Another drink?

Uh yes… *(sigh)*

<Nyer tva whiska, pallo.>

<Nyer tva? Hmph.

Zee gontay buya glugo?>

<Zyek. Talma bootet.>

Know what, it's good to actually get out
and *see* this part of Europe.

Hotel. TV studio. Gig. Airport.

Gig. Radio station. Gig.

'Mr McCann, what do you think represents the sound of Scotland?'
'Police sirens. Next question.'

So I'm sitting there in yet another hotel bar,
watching yet another match involving two European teams
I know absolutely nothing about except
their names don't rhyme with *anything*,
and I thought: know what?
See for just one night?
I want to get a bit…
closer to things.
Smell the *truth* of a country, know?

                    You will smell that here.

Em. What country are we actually in again?

                    You are very funny for Britishman.
Scotsman.

                    To me is same.

Not to me.
Anyway, thanks for coming out tonight.

                    Is job.

Aye, but I appreciate it.
There's probably things you'd
rather be doing instead
of hanging out with a client.
I mean, are you not married?

                    My wife…she used to it.
                    Before, I was in army. So this
                    more preference to her.

You were in the army?
What was that like?

                    Let us say is better working for record
                    company than fighting war.

I can imagine.

No. You cannot.

Well, Miko? Here's to survival

What did you survive?

The tour.

(sigh)
Okay. *Slainte*?

Slainte indeed!
Aah!

gnmp

Burns, doesn't it?

Like Rabbie!

Ha ha, good one.
Anyway, were you no gonnay
put the jukebox on?

Yes.

<jukey no vorka?>

<gie eet a dunto>

<ah>

Now, this track, this band,
very good guitar. You listen.

Yeah! Turbo folk!
The sound of the people, eh Miko?
Cannay beat it, whatever country you're in.

<Ak. Blethereen gay.
Zut! Zut!>

Shit.

What's that?

<Soko nervista. Dane ma heid in, pallo.>

I don't. Speak. Your language.
What's he saying?

                    He's just wondering if you
                    can keep it down so he can
                    hear the song?

Oh aye, sure, no problem.

                    <Excusa. Touristaz, ken?
                    Numpty.
                    Dane ma heid in tay!>
                                        <Britiz?>

          <Scottiz.>

                              <Iz zame heeng, naw?>

          <Zyet.>

                              <Breetez. Poofay poofay.
                              Teesh ma shyeert?
                              Naw!
                              Nae wey.>

          <Oka.>

What's he saying?

                    We are just conversing about this band.
                    He doesn't like their new album.

He seems pretty angry about it.

                    He is a big fan.

I remember when I used to feel like that about music.
Saw U2 at Celtic Park. 1993. I was only fifteen.
All those thousands of people. And one man,
just one man, controlling what they thought,
what they felt.

                    Yes, we have had that here.

U2 played in this country?

No.

Anyway, I saw him standing there,
this tiny figure on a stage.
Everyone just…giving themselves to him.
And I thought: the power of that.

<Bono zavez vurld.>

Perhaps now we should concentrate
on the song?

You'll never feel as passionately about music
as you do when you're fifteen.

When I was fifteen.
Hm.

<Lit! You tva bawbags.
Yappa yappa.
Kveed!>

<Excusa.>

Good song eh!

<Vit?>

Turbo folk! Big thumbs up!

<Vit yappa?>

Cool shirt!
What it's made from…?

<Zay teesh ma shyeert!
Hofannay.>

<Tourista, ken?>

<Bvat bvat smacko doof!>

<I zpika tay him.>

<Yat! Lasto varneen.>

Wow, he's really passionate about that band.

> Listen,
> you should stop the touching of his shirt.

But did you tell him I like the shirt?
That's what I'm trying to communicate to him.

> He is not interested. He just warn
> you to stop touching it.

He *warned* me?
Oh no no, he's got it all wrong.

> No, I would leave. Serious.

Listen, pal.

> <Zar?>

I didn't mean anything by it.
Only touched your shirt as a compliment.
No hassle here.

> <Votto?>

> <Shyeert coolio.>

> <Zay poofta?>

> <Um. Mebbes. Em…
> lika Ziggy Stardoost?>

> <Hyem?>

> <Bi?>

> <Aska aska!>

What's he saying?

> He says he want to know if you have
> sex with another man in the ass?

Um.
I mean, I don't know him very well,
so uh…

He is not making proposition.
You understand?
He is angry, like wasp.

Oh, I see.
Then I think it's best if you tell him no.

<Naw poofta.>

<Goot!
Tello him glug glug
maka mya steeeemboats.>

He wants you to buy him drink.

Uh. Sure.
What would he like?

<Scottiz vhiska!>

He wants you to make selection of
The Scottish whisky that is the most mwah!
Special.

Most special! No problem.

<Ziska buddy? Neebor? Pallo?>

<Gotta loombared.
Geez a break!>

<Ha ha ha>

Uh, sorry to interrupt.
Will this also be covered by the record company?

None of this is paid for by record company.

So who pays for it?

I do.

Ah, Miko…I'd help you out
but I don't have any currency.
Usually the marketing guys always…
y'know?

<Zar....eejit....>

So I suppose I must pay for this also?

If you could. Um.
Just get him one of the cheap ones.
He won't know.

<Vhiska. Grantz.>

Fine country you have here!

<Vatta yaboo the noo?>

<Gon mental zi coontra.>

<Ha! Zo. Gon mental zi coontra?
Hyam Britiz.
Simbat wiv zat,
Solla vocho cho cho
heed the baw?
Gava boom
bang
Deedo.>

He says thank you.

Ah, no problem.
Anytime! Cheers!

<Huh. Chyiz.
Britiz. Scottiz.
Zey keel.
Zey keel.
Myoooordoraaaaaaz.>

He's really fired up.
What was all that about?

Oh, is nothing.
He is merely pointing out that you
British only stopped occupying
this country thirteen years ago.

Really?

                    Yes. During the 'peacekeeping'

                    <Familia? Vorjack?>

                                        <Zyet.>

                    in which some of his family were killed.
                    That sort of thing.

Oh. Um.

                    Do not worry. Long time ago.

                                      Not for me.

Do you…
Do you speak English?

                                            No.

                                      heh heh

                    Ah! This also good song.

What's it called?

                    Is called
                    'She Leave Me So I Shoot Her'

That right, aye?

                    Is very passionate love song.

Very passionate.

                                  <Shya lyav meeee
                                  Zo I shyeot hoir!>

                    <Zat crazy beetcho.>

                                  <Takka zee kyeedz>

                    <Takka zee doyg>

                                <Woof woof!>

                    <Shya lyav meeeee>

<Zo I shyeot hoir!>

Um.

<Zyen?>

<Nineteen Ninety Three!>

Guys?

<Shya lyav meeeee>

<Zo I shyeot hoir!>

I'm just going to the toilet.

Okay.

You couldn't…
get me another drink?

<RAT A-TAT A-TAT>

<RAT-AT AT-AT AT-AT AT-AT>

Actually I'm fine.

(exits)

I miss that soft, sweet
woman…

Sooooo much.

Ha ha ha ha ha.

Heh heh.

It's a good song.

From the heart.

Listen, friend.
My companion, the Scotsman,
He doesn't have a clue,
But he means no harm.

What is he *doing* in here?

Doesn't he know what kind of place this is?

He sees only our native hospitality.

Are we in a hospital?

No.

So I ask again: what's he doing here?

He's on tour.

Tour? Of duty?

No no, not *that* kind of tour.
He is a famous singer
over in Scotland.

But he's not in Scotland though, is he?
Which is the problem with
the last lot of them who were here.
They were in *our* country.

That has nothing to do with him.

What are you even doing with this clown?

Officially? I am helping him
'discover our culture'.

Unofficially?

It looks like I am helping him
to get drunk.

Is that so? Well.
I am all for strengthening relations
with our European brothers.

Please.
This is my livelihood.
You know how things were after the war,
it took me a long time to *get* a job like this.
We are not looking for trouble.

I'm sure those British soldiers

who took over this very bar
with their drunken songs
and their beatings for anyone
who dared to ask them
why they were here were
not looking for trouble.

But they found it.

This is all in the past.
It is people like you who
will not let our country
move forwards,
become whole again.

Know something, friend?
I'm sure I recognise you from somewhere.
Where did you grow up?

Graatz.

Near the Zhetyn farm?

Yes.

I remember.
They called you the Little Cobra.

You're thinking of someone else.

Because of your *eyes*.
No.

Look at me.

Leave me alone.

Look at me.

Fuck off!

Ah. It *is* you.
There's that famous temper.

Listen, *comrade*.
Now I work for a record company.

Good job. Nice wife. Own home.
That might sound gay to you and your
brothers, but I went through
the same shit as the rest of you did.

I've had enough.

So I'm asking you, please,
let's not go back there.

                                                 Hmm.
                        Now you are bringing this
                        'singer'. *Their* culture-

It's just music.

                          – to our homeland?

                            My friend,
                   you can wear their T-shirt,
          but you'll always be one of us.

Hey.

                              <Ziko.
                   Vilcom! Howya dane?>

Hey. My main man!

                  <Zuska dronko glug glug?
                      Gatta pished!>

What?

He want to buy you drink.
To thank you for your earlier
generosity.

                              <Scottiz!>

One from your homeland.

Aw, thanks mate.

                          <Zutto problama.
                       Fire in neebor.>

See? I'd heard that about this country,
that your hospitality was very Scottish.

                                                    <Heh?>

We are friendly nation too!

                                                    <Zyit?>

                    <Janta. Scottiz pallo veka
                    'all nations'.>

                                                    <Pallo?>

                        Ha ha ha ha ha ha HA HA HA
                              Ha HA HA HA HA
                                            hee
                                            hee

Everything okay?

                                                    hee
                                                    hee

                    Yes, he like your Scottish humour.

Ah, I see. We're well known for that,
our gallusness.
That's why every country loves us
and hates the English.

That and our music, of course.

                                <Ah. Zyee moozik.
                                       Scottiska?
                                    Yordaz playa?>

                    He wants to know if you play.

Oh?
Well, heh. I do have a certain
reputation in my home country.

                                                    <Yook.

                                        Playay ze Turbo Volk
                                                vitta zoska.>

                    <Zerioosko?>

                                        <Gotta latta gittar.
                                                Vill sort oot.>

Where's he going?

                    He has guitar.
                    He want you to sing song.

He wants me to..?
No, I'm here incognito tonight.
I want to get away from all of that.

                                        <Zisk! Zisk!
                    Famoosa Scottiz sangar.>

                    He is impressed by your fame.

Is he, aye?

                                        <Heera.>

                    Can you play?

You want a quick…?

Oh well.
Maybe just one, eh?

Ooh nice guitar.
is it in tune…?
yeah?

                                        <Scottizka Turbo Volk!>

                    Can you play Scottish music?

Right.
This is from my new album, *Peach Melba*.
It's about a guy who loves a girl
but she doesn't love him back.

It's called 'Nothing Hurts…Except the Pain'

Hoooo, baby…

> <Akak! Baws! Scottizka Turbo!>

No, he not want to hear one
of *your* songs.

He want to hear 'traditional'.
The real music.

Let us know the Scottish peoples.

> <zyaaaaar>

Ah, got ye. Let me think…

Okay. This one's called 'Bonnie Dundee'.
It's a regimental march.

> <Arma chanto.
> Trat trat trat trat.>

> <Scottiz arma? Ek!
> Tikeen pish?>

How does it go…? Em.

Tae the Lords o convention twas Claverhouse spoke
E'er the King's Crown go down there are crowns to be broke
So each cavalier who loves honour and me
Let him follow the bonnets o Bonnie Dundee.

Come fill up my cup, come fill up can
Come saddle my horses and call out my men
Unhook the West Port and let us gae free
For it's up with the bonnets o' Bonnie Dundee

> <Scuza. Hey.
> Niy niy niy.>

What's the matter?

> <Arma chanto?>

This is song of army?

Aye. Scots Guards.

<Aska. Skottizk Arma? Tsh!>

Were you in Scottish military?

No, but my Uncle Tam was.
He used to sing this to me and my brothers,
made us march up and down the room,
saluting him.

I was high on Ribena. Loved it.

<Familia chanto.
Arma chanto.

Seenga laka
pwoofh! pwoofh!

teet teet teet
eee eee eee>

Ha ha ha.

What's so funny?

He says you sing like small girl.

Excuse me?

Song for army marching?
About family? Blood?
Fighting enemy of homeland?

You sing like small girl

<weeva>

with

<Swish! Swish!>

pigtails.

Is that right?

Aye, well. Listen.
The pair ay yese.
My uncle served in the army
for twenty-five year. Proudly.

Fought in Argentina and Belfast.

<Zo?>

Zo! Listen to his song, right?

<Maka mya belyev.>

Make him believe.

Aye, I understood that just fine, Miko.
Yese think I'm no uptay it?

Want me to keep going? Aye. Good.

Dundee he is mounted and rides up the street
The bells tae ring backwards, the drums tae are beat
But the provost douce man he says, 'Just let it be.'
When the toon is well rid o' that devil Dundee.

Come fill up my cup, come fill up can
Come saddle my horses and call out my men
Unhook the West Port and let us gae free
For it's up with the bonnets o' Bonnie Dundee

<Et. Et.>

<Pf.>

Whit is it noo?

<Saya maka mya belyev.>

You said you would make him bel-

Believe. Aye. I heard him.
Listen, mate.
You know I've played the Main Stage
at T in the Park?

(shrug)   (shrug)

The. Main. Stage.

(shrug)   (shrug)

Aye awright,
it was at half two in the afternoon.
But still! Ken?
fuckin

There are hills beyond Pentland and lands beyond Forth
Be there lords in the south, there are chiefs in the north
There are brave downie wassles three thousand times three
Cry hey for the bonnets o' Bonnie Dundee

<Bettoro…>

<Brava brava!>

Come fill up my cup, come fill up my can
Come saddle my horses and call out my men
Unhook the West Port and let us gae free
For it's up with the bonnets o'

<Bonniez Dunday!>

Then awa tae the hill to the lee and the rocks
Ere I own a usurper I'll crouch with the fox
So tremble false wigs in the midst of yer glee
For you've no seen the last of my bonnets and me

Come fill up my cup.

<Come feyl up my kyan!>

Come saddle my horses.

<Aynd kaal out my myen!>

Unhook the West Port.

<Eh let uz giz freeeeeeee>

For it's   up   with   the   bonnets   o   Bonnie   Dundee

                                        <Ya dansa!
                                        Brav brav!>

                    He is very impressed.
                    I am too.

Aye. Just as well.

                                        <Ye myka mya belyev.>

I made him believe?

                    Yes. If only the NME could see
                    you now eh?

Too right. Aye.
Stick *that* up yer Asda.

                                        <Skotsa. Eh? Brav.>

Scotland the Brave.
Aye, ye're welcome.
Ye want me tay sing somethin else?

                    No.   No.

Right. Well. Thanks for the lennay the guitar.
Quite enjoyed that. Whoof! No felt like that for a while.

                    Ah.
                    I so glad we is all now friends.

                    <Comrado?>

                                        <….comrado…>

                    yes uh
                    I believe it is…my round.
                    As you say in Britain!

Scotland.

                    Yes, Scotland.

                                        <Skotska. Goot.>

Scotland. Good. Aye.

I'm glad you agree.
A proud people, ken?
Don't like to see our heritage *mocked*.

                                               heh heh

Ken whit, Miko?
I'll have a double whisky.

                    A…double.

                                   <Dooblo?>

                    <Tva TVA vhiksa…>

                                   <Ah. Nae probz.
Skotska muzyak.
Mwah! Mwah!
Brava.>

You like that, aye?

                                   <Aaaaaaay…>

Aaaaaaaay….

Ha ha ha.

                                   Heh heh heh.
<Arma?>

Eh?

                              <Arma? Bang bang?>

Oh right.
No, I wis never in the army.
UNCLE.
Scots. Guards.
Never mind.
Were you ever in the army?

                              <Eh? Ma arma?>

Aye. Were you…bang bang?

<Ah. Yisk.
                    Nineteen nineties.>

Nineteen nineties. Ah.
That's when the British were occupying this place?

Still though.
I heard youse were uptay aw sortsay
dodgy shit round here, eh?

Heh heh heh.

                                        <Vit?>

                    What did you say?

I'm just saying likes.
Heh heh.
If yese werenay uptay anythin
we wouldnay have been here, would we?

                    <Akk!>

Naughty naughty!
Heh heh heh.

                                        <gvvvvvv>

                    And what do you know of this?

Ho. Hang on, I'm just kiddin yese on.

                    What age were you?

Back then? Dunno.
Fifteen or sixteen.

                    <Sezis vanka!>

                    Do you know what I was doing
                    when I was fifteen?

Naw, eh…

                    I was in militia unit, protecting
                    hills around my father's farm

from enemy who wanted to kill us.
I was night patrol
because my eyesight.

On the farm we had rat.
And because I such *skill* at spotting rat.
They called me Little Cobra.
I
see
you

Yaaaagh!

!!!

When *you* were fifteen-

<teet teet teet teet.>

You were in love with
pop stars.

Heh heh heh.

Aye?
Well. Listen.
Bono's a man who made stadium
rock into a new artform.
He's no a *pop star*.

<Zay?>

<Ha ha. Zyez. Bono zeela
rocka stadyoom Picasso.>

<Oh! Mezybez Michael Jackson
eza la Malcolm X?>

Aye, and I'm sure in this country
youse aw understaun aboot music,
hammerin fuckin sheet metal aw day.
Ya coupla bastards.

Whaur's that double whisky?

Here.

Finally!

Slainte.

fuckin
Had a gid wee laugh at ma expense,
have yese, Miko?

No, sir, ha ha.
It is not like that.

gnmp
Yes.

Aye, well. Know whit?

Please. Is fine. We all just make joke.

This is a fuckin shite country.

Heh heh heh.

Yer food's rotten.

Sir. Please, calm down.

Yer women are mingin.

That is enough now, please-

And I know fine well what happened here,
ya bunch of murderin bast-

HO.

ek!
miko
kf
ek
cannay
breathe
let me go

Of course.

jesus

heh

gasp

wheeze

cough

(beep)

<Hallo? Ja. Isis here.
Za Breeteesh manna yappa yap
veziz myordoraz.
Scoom.
Oza…
Em. Lama theenko.>

…fuckin maniacs…

<Oka.

Tekit ootside.

Ovnat.
Click click.
Deedo.>

(beep)

<Yisk?>

<Ja.>

Excuse me.
I go outside.
Need fresh air.

(exits)

Cough

<Vhiksa.>

                             Whisky?

\<Ja.\>

                          No problem.
                             Enjoy.

\<Throatska gek gek.
Miko zuppa tay hi doh.
Kalaka.
Meh canno breffo!
Youzay gon geez gid dooan?
Meh tourista ken?
No kenna bettaro neebor.\>

                      So we are murderers.

\<Myord...?\>

                      Murderers, aye.

\<Myordoraaz?
Niy niy. Listo.
Le Breetesh govamun
Zay yappa yappa.
Tokka zay
"Oh izza commyoonisto.
Comrade comrade. Bang bang.
Evel."\>

                             Evil?
                      We are...evil?

\<*Za* zaya evel. Govamun!
Ve gontay do eh?
Zay yappa.
Propa za ganda.
Ve belevska.\>

                      Belevska?

\<Ja. Belevska?\>

Believe…?
Ah, I see you *believed* your government.

<Za?>

The sweet little fairy stories you British people are told
by your leaders,
of innocent Red Riding Hood
and the Big Bad Wolf.

<Volf?>

Wolf. Aaargh.

<ek>

This country is not innocent, no.
You have seen that already.
No one who fought in that war
can remain truly innocent.

But your country?
Your country fought in that war too.
So you cannot be Little Red Riding Hood either.
Do you believe *that*?

<Belevska!
Lookeh.
Zi joosta playa moozik>.

Music?

<Moozikso.>

Ah, but this music you play.
This music is not innocent.

<Moozika moozika!
Peach Melba noomero tyen.
Justa vonto bya lakka lakka
Yoo! Too!
Lakka ze Celtic Parka!>

Sorry, what?

Sel. Teec. Parka.

<Eh. Bigga geegzo.
Rocka rolla geegzo.
Za stadyoom!
Cameron McCann!
Gonza big man!
Gon yersel. Ho!>

What are you talking about?

<Plez. Jusa mooziko.>

Music. Yes, what about it?

<Belyev.>

Believe?

<Ja! Mooziko belyev.
Kem feel up my kep.>

sigh
Okay then, my friend.
Come on. One last time.
For the road.

Come fill up my can.

<Yaaz!
Komm saddelo horzez.>

and call out my men.

<*Zun hook le West Portz.*>

And let us gae free

<*Foriz up wiz bonneto!*

O Bonnie Dundeeeeeee.

<Oh. Byootizful.
Zats ma hame.>

68

Your home?

<Dundez. Ayez. Neebor country.>

Dundee? Home?

<Hame.>

I see.
Well, Scotsman.
This place is *my* home.
And I did not invite you in.

Come.

Miko.
Please. Don't. I didn't mean
anything by it.

<Zereko kaka.
Vatcheet.>

<Za. Heeren ya.>

Sir. I apologise for
my violent conduct earlier.
It was most unprofessional.
Please forgive, sir.

Don't worry about it, Miko.
I probably pushed it a wee bit myself.
And it definitely feels weird you
still calling me sir.

Ken, after you tried to choke me an that?

<Yiska ootside.>

<Ja.>

<Vyo?>

<Jaaaaaaa.>

<Draga kalashna.>

Can we maybe…
Can we maybe go?
Now that I've, y'know,
seen your country?

                    I do not think that would be wise.

Why not?

                    Outside. There is people.

Oh no.
Is it the paparazzi?
They've tracked me down?

                                        heh heh heh

            Yes.

Suppose there are fans out there as well?

            They uh.
            They know you are here.

You sure it's me they want?

            They ask for the 'Britishman'.

Oh well. So much for being off-duty.
Wonder how Bono copes with this.

Shall we run the gauntlet then?

            I will stay in bar.
            Few moments.

Aye sure, finish your drink.
Listen. No hard feelings guys, eh?

                                    <Vit?>

I said: no hard feelings?

                                    <Naw.
                            Scool neebor.>

Hey, if you want to come to the gig tomorrow night.
I'll dedicate a song to youse.

<Zong?>

A song. A SONG.

<Ah vonto songa?
Von lasto teem…

<Shya lyav meeee!>

<Zo I shyeot hoir!>

Ha ha. Quality tune.

<Zat crazy beetcho.>

Might cover it on the next record.
Thinking about a concept album.
About the two sides of my personality.
Maybe call it 'Milk Chocolate/Dark Chocolate'

<Takka zee kyeedz.>

<Takka zee dog!>

<Woof woof.>

C'mon, Miko.

<Shya lyav meeee!>

<Zo I shyeot haar!>

Ha ha. Okay see ya, guys.
You've been the best crowd of the tour.
But I have a free digital download to promote.

<She lyaav me.>

<Zo I shyeot hoir!>

Now open the door. Elvis is ready to leave the building.

RAT A-TAT A-TAT A-TAT A-TAT A-TAT A-
TAT A-TAT A-TAT A-TAT A-TAT A-TAT A-TAT A-

TAT A-TAT A-TAT A-TAT A-TAT A-TAT A-TAT A-
TAT A-TAT A-TAT A-TAT A-TAT A-TAT A-TAT A-
TAT A-TAT A-TAT A-TAT A-TAT A-TAT A-TAT
A-TAT A-TAT A-TAT A-TAT A-TAT A-

END